T0209737

ALIA'S VISION

First Transformation

Kianna Smith

BALBOA.
PRESS

A DIVISION OF HAY HOUSE

Balboa Press books may be ordered through booksellers or by contacting:

Balboa Press
A Division of Hay House
1663 Liberty Drive
Bloomington, IN 47403
www.balboapress.com
1 (877) 407-4847

Because of the dynamic nature of the Internet, any web addresses or links contained in
this book may have changed since publication and may no longer be valid. The views
expressed in this work are solely those of the author and do not necessarily reflect the
views of the publisher, and the publisher hereby disclaims any responsibility for them.

The author of this book does not dispense medical advice or prescribe the use of any
technique as a form of treatment for physical, emotional, or medical problems without the
advice of a physician, either directly or indirectly. The intent of the author is only to offer
information of a general nature to help you in your quest for emotional and spiritual well-
being. In the event you use any of the information in this book for yourself, which is your
constitutional right, the author and the publisher assume no responsibility for your actions.

Any people depicted in stock imagery provided by Getty Images are models,
and such images are being used for illustrative purposes only.
Certain stock imagery © Getty Images.

Print information available on the last page.

ISBN: 978-1-9822-2190-4 (sc)
ISBN: 978-1-9822-2192-8 (hc)
ISBN: 978-1-9822-2191-1 (e)

Library of Congress Control Number: 2019901709

Balboa Press rev. date: 03/26/2019

CONTENTS

Prologue

Leaving Home

Alia was standing on a street corner with her adopted brother, Alee. It was just the two of them. Alia didn't know what to say. They were running away from their home. They didn't know where they would go. There was frightful fighting where they lived but her family was safe so far. Alee had no family other than hers. They had protected him many years ago when his parents were killed. They both looked at each other, and suddenly they knew where to go. So, they walked.

They were walking away from the fighting and away from the war which had harmed so many people. They wanted to find another way, a place of peace and joy and serenity. They were very sad, very sad. Many of their friends were physically scarred from the fighting. Many folks were dead.

Alia and Alee wanted PEACE.

They walked away from the fighting and stress.

They were surrounded by beautiful, tall trees. The sound of the fighting became less. There was no way they could convince her family to go with them. They had tried. Her family didn't understand—even why Alia and Alee chose to leave. Alee was not even of their tribe.

Alia was 18 years old, now; Alee was 22.

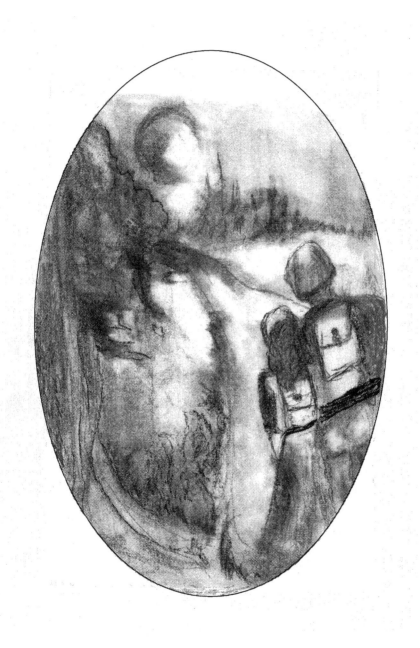

Alia and Alee Leave Home

Night was all around them.

Most people were sleeping in their homes, or at least trying to sleep. Alia and Alee were walking away from what they had always known.

Suddenly they were blessed by the moon in the night sky, a very beautifully bright moon. The moon was pointing the direction where they needed to go.

Finally, it was very, very dark.

With a blanket and coats, they crawled through some trees because Alia was very tired. Surprisingly, they felt very safe.

Alee found a safe spot for them now. It was quite hidden. He spread the lush thick blanket. Alia laid on the blanket and was asleep as soon as her eyes closed.

Alee saw the moonlight appearing above the trees. He quietly wondered to himself.

"What is our next step".

Soon Alee was also deeply ASLEEP.

CHAPTER 1

OBI

In her dream, Alia found herself in a different place. The place seemed to be very quiet. it was so peaceful. Everything and everywhere was peaceful and very quiet.

She saw a unicorn, a horse with a horn on his forehead. The unicorn looked at Alia, but he would not come close to her. He suddenly galloped off into the forest.

The sky had brilliantly colored birds with huge wing spans and many delightful colors. Each bird had their own song.

Hearing the song, Alia felt even more peaceful.

Among the butterflies and flowers, all colors of blues, reds, greens, purples, violets, and yellows, could be seen. Each butterfly touched the flowers lightly, and lovingly.

Such incredible beauty, Alia felt deep peace in her heart once more.

Suddenly she could see a tiny puppy staring at her, wanting to come forward, but waiting for her invitation. It was very frisky and a gold-beige color. This puppy knew Alia as she knelt down, and he skipped immediately into her arms. Alia touched his fluffy hair. He was so happy and eager to be with her, he sniffed her face. She cuddled the puppy and laughed.

Alia felt no longer alone. With the puppy in her arms Alia looked at her hands, feet and clothes and she was suddenly much younger, perhaps 12 years old. Her hair was almost to her waist.

She couldn't understand why, but she felt very good.

It was sunny and clear. Everything was lovely. She Looked ahead and saw a lake with sparkling blue water. Butterflies, birds, even some frisky rabbits. She felt peace in her heart with all the animals around her.

Then Alia saw a strange 'being'. A fuzzy being about three feet tall. He was looking at her now. Alia didn't feel fear for herself. The 'fuzzy being' was just looking at her. She didn't fear him. She was perplexed and knew he was a 'he.' He stayed still where he was looking at Alia.

She decided, "I'll walk toward the lake." So, she did.

The sky was magnetically blue. She felt love and she loved everything, the beautiful area, the puppy and the new-found 'fuzzy being'.

She kept walking towards the lake and the 'fuzzy being' was closer to her now. They looked at each other occasionally. "I wonder how to communicate with him. Can we both understand what each other is saying?"

She walked further. The grass was very green everywhere. And the flowers were so many colors! Everything was incredibly beautiful. The lake was closer now.

She believed this was a magical place.

Now the 'fuzzy being' walked with her and her puppy. The 'fuzzy being' seemed human-like. Maybe—kind of a human. He was standing straight, like humans do. They stopped for a moment and looked at each other. She came a bit closer to him, and he came closer to her. All of a sudden, they were face-to-face. Alia didn't feel afraid of him, and he was not afraid of her. They were very interested in each other.

Suddenly, the puppy wants to be released. The puppy skips over to the 'fuzzy being'. The puppy jumps into the 'fuzzy being's' arms and licks his face. Quickly, the puppy jumps down, circles the 'fuzzy being', and runs off into the nearby forest.

The puppy is about LOVE, Alia knows now. She'll see him again and feels very sure about this fact.

Alia finally asked the 'fuzzy being' a question. "Can you understand me?" What came from his mouth sounded like, "Obi ute. Obi ute." Alia said, "All right, can you speak a little slower? I'll speak slowly too."

Strangely enough, the 'fuzzy being' spoke slowly.

Not English, but "Obi ute" meant "I am Obi."

Somehow, Alia now knew what he was saying. She spoke back, "I am Alia. I am Alia." "Alia is your name. Is that what you are called?"

Alia laughing said, "Yes, it's my name." First, it took some effort to understand Obi's language, Alia and the 'fuzzy being' finally understood each other's languages.

Obi was very important. Alia wasn't sure why Obi was important. She didn't understand why, but Obi was her guide.

She could communicate with Obi now. He could communicate with her. He was telling her to go into the blue lake water now.

Alia replied, "No!!! I don't know how to swim."

Obi

Obi replied, "I'll teach you to go under the water easily now."

Alia said. "This scares me. I'm afraid. This land is heart-warming, but I'm afraid of the blue lake. I'm afraid of the water."

Obi said, "I'll teach you. You'll have no problems in the water of the blue lake."

Alia said, "You may bring other people here and promise to teach them, and they die."

Obi said, "You won't die. I know how to swim. We'll go very deep and you'll be pleased. You will meet a merman who is a very wonderful being."

Alia said. "I'm afraid and not ready to go."

Obi gently said, "In the beginning, we'll swim on top of the water. Easy and gentle. We'll go a little bit at a time."

Alia said, "I don't know. Let's go walking the land."

Obi replied, "All right. When you are ready, I'll teach you how to swim."

Alia said, "Okay. We'll see." And she walked quickly away from the blue lake water. Obi still believed she needed to go into the blue lake water—into the deep blue water.

Because she would find important answers to her unspoken questions. Obi knew she was afraid of the water and she just couldn't do anything else.

They saw the mountain and it was beautiful, immense and very close. Alia said, "I think we should climb the mountain."

Obi said, "All right. Let's go. We'll climb the mountain."

Chapter 2

Wandering

It took a while. It was a pretty big mountain. Maybe not as big as Mt. Everest at her home. They climbed and they climbed for hours. They got to the top of the mountain, and they were very tired and hungry. Very, very hungry. They looked around. Alia looked at the sky. It was so clear and crisp.

Obi looked around also and found a cave. He thought it might be best for them to spend the night in the cave. Alia looked at him. The cave was dark, but she was more willing to go into the unknown cave than into the water of the blue lake. She followed Obi, and they entered the cave. It was a shallow cave, but it was warm inside—much warmer than it was outside.

Amazingly enough, there was food there for them. They didn't know how it happened, but there was food. It was a certain type of food that Obi ate, which was different from the type of food Alia ate. The food was a porridge in bowls and it was very warm. Amazing! And there was cool clean water, too in cups. Alia was surprised. Obi just accepted things as they were.

Then he said, "Now, we need to be quiet." So, they sat on the ground and became very still and quiet.

It got darker at night.

Alia sat next to Obi. "I'm a little cold."

Obi made a space for Alia, "I've got a lot of fuzzy fur. Sit very close to me and we'll go to sleep."

Alia sat very close to Obi. They were near the edge of the cave. It was comfortable. Alia said, "All right. I'll just close my eyes now." Obi answered, "All right."

So, they slept really well. At least Alia felt really rested when she woke up the next morning. She looked outside the cave, at the sun as it was very slowly opening its eyes, getting ready for the morning.

And Obi woke up too and then he stood beside Alia. Obi looked and incredible peace surrounded them.

Alia felt like in some way, she was home. She didn't know why, but she felt peaceful.

She felt as though she was at her true home, finally.

All of a sudden, three little beings were scampering around just inside the cave. They didn't look human, they looked more like little bears. They came scampering through the cave opening. The first being stayed on the ground. The second being hopped up on the first one's shoulder. The third being hopped on the second one's shoulder. All three were together now. Together they were as tall as Obi. They picked up all the dishes and left.

Alia cried, "Wait! Who are you? You left us the food. We thank you." As they were all on top of each other's shoulders, they bowed forward and said, "You're welcome,"

We are called "The Magnificents."

Alia's eyes sparkled when she laughing said "Thank you very much."

The Magnificents

Now, Alia could understand their language, just as she could understand Obi's language. She didn't know how it happened, but she could understand the Magnificents language. Amazingly enough, they could understand her language. It was strange, but wonderful. She'd used the word "wonderful" so often now, but she felt very wonderful.

The Magnificents—they looked very different. They had big eyes and big, pointy ears. They had fur all over their bodies and wore short pants with white shirts. Alia thought they were probably boys, but she didn't know exactly.

They disappeared and immediately reappeared carrying breakfast for Alia and Obi. It was porridge with honey and more water.

Alia loved it.

The Magnificents said, "It's very important to drink water. Very important." The top little being hopped down, and then the next one hopped down, and each was now a foot tall. They began spinning, and they were spinning and spinning and suddenly disappeared.

Alia turned to Obi and said, "They were so nice."

Things are quiet now, and Alia said, "We should go down the mountain now."

Obi said, "All right."

So, very carefully, they began climbing down the mountain.

It took them some time to get the bottom of the mountain. It was in the early afternoon.

The land was very quiet. They couldn't even hear the birds. It was so very quiet.

CHAPTER 3

A DECISION

"Things are so quiet." Alia was feeling 'odd' inside herself. She didn't feel happy. Alia felt as though she was waiting for something or someone to appear. She didn't know exactly why she was waiting.

She asked Obi about her feeling. "Do feel you are waiting for someone or something?"

Obi said, "Things are very quiet here."

Alia replied, "It's not like the happiness that I felt yesterday. Nothing is moving, nothing is breathing, it seems as though, nothing is alive. I don't understand it."

Obi said, "Are you ready to go under the blue lake water now?"

"No! I'm not ready to go under the water now. No. No. No." It was just so quiet. "Perhaps if we go someplace else, perhaps it will be different. Let's go to the forest and see if there's anything alive in there."

Obi said, "All right, let's go."

They walked to the forest. As they are walking, Alia hears no birds, sees no flowers. It's as if nothing is alive. They walked a while, and finally they were inside the forest. It was very strange again. It was still quiet, but there was the wind. She could hear the wind blowing through the trees. She thought it was beautiful. Just the wind.

They walked further into the forest. It became darker because there were so many trees and there was the sound of the wind.

Alia turned to Obi and said, "Does this seem strange? Does this seem strange to you at all?"

Obi said, "It's very, very quiet."

It was getting near to dinner time. She said, "I'm getting hungry." Immediately they saw "The Magnificents". The same three little beings—a foot tall each and they gave Alia and Obi cheese sandwiches to eat. Alia welcomed them. They handed the sandwiches and cups of water to Alia and Obi. Then Magnificents left like whirling dervishes.

"Don't you think that was kind of strange? They were somewhat different this morning."

Obi just sighed.

They ate their food. It was delicious. Alia was so grateful to have the food and they drank some of their water.

Alia said "Let's walk on." They walked through the entire forest. It was a quiet, calm forest with lots of trees. They were fir trees and very old. Alia again seemed to sense the beautiful blue water of the lake.

Finally, Alia looked at Obi and said, "I am so tired. Let's go under this tree and rest."

They slept for a few hours.

Upon waking, Alia spoke, "Now, I positively need to go into the blue lake water."

Obi says, "Very well. We have waited for a long time for the blue lake water. It's perfectly okay. Your answers for yourself and for others are there."

He turned to her, and he said, "Just go into the blue lake water now." "I'm suddenly very afraid," Alia said.

Obi said, "Look who is waiting for you? It's the merman in the blue lake now. He'll guide you and make it easy to go into water. He will always take care of you."

Obi promised, "I AM always here waiting for your return from blue lake waters."

Chapter 4

The Merman

Alia looked, and she saw a young man. He was probably about four or five years older than her. And when she looked again, the young man was partly like a fish, at least from his belly on downward. His face was very handsome.

Alia said, "You look so familiar to me."

He laughed for he was the merman waiting for Alia. "Come into the water."

Alia was afraid but bit by bit went into the water. When she got deep enough, the merman said, "Get on my back and I will take you deeper into the water very carefully. You'll see."

"I won't be able to breath under the water," Alia said.

With a soft voice the merman gently said, "Don't worry. I want you to hold your breath as we go under the water and don't think about anything. You'll be okay. I promise you'll be okay. Just go into the water with me. You'll see. Just be at peace now."

So, Alia climbed onto his back. She hugged him because that was the only way she was going to stay on his back, and they went into the water. The blue lake was so very beautiful. She could open her eyes. The water tasted a little salty. She no longer needed to breathe. She felt very alive. She loved being in the blue water on the merman's back. Although, she did not want to go off on her own. Never swimming in the water alone. Alia went into the water on the back of the young merman and she loved it. She didn't have to breathe or think about anything.

The Merman, Alia and the Whale

As the merman swam forward, she just noticed the lovely assortment of all the fish. The colors were so golden and vibrant. They went deeper, and she noticed unusual fish— all different colors. They went deeper, and saw this huge fish, a whale. It was as big as a submarine and black colored.

Alia asked, "Do you see the humongous black whale?"

The merman said, "Yes. Do you see that the whale is coming towards us?"

All Alia could think, "Oh my God. I guess this is the end of my story."

But, it didn't happen. What she feels now is Peace and Serenity, a wonderful love inside.

The whale is very, very big.

The merman said to the whale "Hello Dearest Friend, it's so good to see you."

The Whale nodded, "Yes. Yes. It's good to see you, too."

Surprised, Alia asked the merman, "Do you know this particular whale?"

The merman said, "No. Peace and Serenity is who we are. If we allowed ourselves to be afraid, the whale would eat us. The Whale now recognizes us as God's messengers."

So, the young merman and Alia waved to the whale and swam past.

The merman said, "Now you must come to the front of my body. It will be easy to do. Then I will hold you under your arms and we'll swim deeper. You will see a white light surrounding us and total darkness outside of us. Don't think about it. For the next part of our journey, we are going through a space of nothingness or darkness. You may feel fear. I AM with you. I AM always your protection. We will be in a circle of light for a while."

Alia said, "I feel so odd."

The merman said, "That's okay. Only feel the light surrounding us. You'll be okay."

Alia said, "I'm afraid of this uneasy feeling."

He said, "Be at PEACE and SERENITY in your heart."

Alia just held PEACE and SERENITY in her heart and climbed to the front of his body. The merman held her arms gently, and they started swimming downward.

Alia said, "You seem familiar to me. Do I know you?". The merman said, "Perhaps."

Alia, "I don't know any person who is also part fish." He said, "I'm not always a merman."

Alia was confused, "Oh." She didn't know what else to say. She remembered PEACE and SERENITY.

I'll stay quiet now and see what happens next.

True to the merman's word, an incredible white light surrounded them. He was holding Alia so carefully in such a way that she was floating. They traveled in the light through the intense darkness. They traveled and traveled with a sense of timelessness.

Alia said, "I'm feeling very sleepy."

The merman smiled and gently replied, "Close your eyes and rest. When you wake up, we'll arrive in Serenity. It's very near, and yet it's very far away. You will like Serenity very much."

Alia couldn't keep her eyes open, so she just floated to sleep. She slept deeply.

All of a sudden, Alia was awake. She found herself lying on a flattened chaise with a young man standing close to her. He has legs! He's not a merman any more. Alia couldn't understand it.

Alia astonished said, "You used to be like a fish! I don't understand it."

He said, "In the water, I become a merman. When I'm out of the water, I become like you. Are you a human?"

"Of course, I'm a human," she said. "Are you human?"

"Not exactly," he said, "but I understand humanity very deeply. I know humans".

CHAPTER 5

SERENITY'S CAEN

The merman said, "We're in Serenity. We're in a place called Serenity."

Alia asked, "Are there other people here? I don't see anybody."

He replied "There are many beings that live here. You will meet some of them. You were in the water and now we have landed in Serenity. Notice that you can breathe now."

Alia replied "Yeah, that's great I can breathe. I don't understand it."

He said, "Yes, you can breathe. In a little while, when you feel up to it, we'll walk around a little bit. I AM always with you. I AM always near you. Only just think of me, and there I AM."

Alia said, "That's a little strange. Just think and you can be right there?"

He replied "That is very true."

Alia said, "Okay. Well, I still feel sleepy.

"Then you must sleep, I AM always with you,"

Alia replied "Well, okay. I'm so sleepy. But I'm glad I can breathe now. I didn't even think of it before you mentioned it. I'm so relieved that I can breathe now."

He gently replied "Good. Just rest. When you awaken, we'll walk around. Maybe you might think about some food to eat. Okay? Sleep well."

And so, she fell asleep deeply with no disturbing memories.

Alia woke up. She looked all around. Her chaise was in a very large room beside the lake. It was like a ballroom, almost.

She felt she was alone, but then she thought of the merman. "What is his name?" she thought." The merman immediately appeared.

He said, "How are you now?"

She said, "Well, I'm very awake now, I feel good." He said, "Did you notice how old you are now?" She thought, I'm not 12 years old anymore.

He said, "You're 18 now." She said, "Where did those other years go?"

He said, "Well, it's difficult to explain. I'll explain a little, and then you will understand more as we go along. Age is something that is an illusion. You are experiencing that illusion, and now you are experiencing the illusion of being 18. It's an illusion. That's basically all I can say now."

Alia said, "I think it's very strange, but I don't feel like 12 years old anymore. It's true. I could feel like 18. I don't know. I just don't understand any of this."

"Remember," he said, "you'll understand more as each day passes. Much more. We welcome you here. We're glad you're here. We'll walk a little bit."

Alia got up very slowly from where she was. She sat up actually, and she put her legs over the end of the chaise lounge. He offered her his hand. She still didn't know his name. She thought, "Okay. I'll learn it later." As she started to walk, she realized she was pretty hungry.

She said so to the merman. "I'm pretty hungry. Can we find food." The merman said, "Let's go to the outer area. There are some tables and someone can take our food order."

They walked slowly down some steps and into Serenity. Alia couldn't see the sun. Things were very light, like walking in sunlight. Down the steps and over to an outside table where they sat down. Sure enough a lovely lady appeared.

Smiling, she said, "My name is Leaf. What would you like to eat?"

Alia said, "What do you have?"

Leaf said, "We have many things. We have a soup. Would that be good?"

Alia said, "Yes. I'm very hungry. I need some vegetables and some soup. And a piece of bread."

Leaf said, "That's perfect. Then she turned to the young man. The merman replied. "I'll have the same as Alia."

Leaf said, "Beautiful choice. I'll bring your food momentarily."

Alia talked to the merman. "What is your real name? I would like to refer to you by your name. Please tell me."

"I'm a merman, as you know, I have a different name under that form. But in this form, you can call me 'Caen'." Alia said, "Caen?"

"Caen is my name. And you are Alia. Is that correct?"

Alia said, "Yes, please call me Alia. And Caen, how old are you?"

For now, he quickly said, "I am older than you. Leaf is bringing our food now."

Bowls of very delicious food arrived. It had many vegetables with a broth that tasted like chicken broth.

Alia said, "Caen, what are these white things in the soup broth?"

He said, "They're like fish, but of course, they're different because we're in Serenity. You will enjoy them very much."

"Are they alive," Alia asked.

"No," said Caen. "Just try them and tell me what you think."

Alia went ahead and ate her soup. It was very delicious. She was surprised. The vegetables looked very similar—not quite the same, but very similar to what she had at home. Now the white things, she couldn't quite understand what they were. She thought they were like a meat or a fish. But, they were tasty! The whole soup was so good, and so was the bread.

The soup actually made Alia feel full. She loved it. Caen ate his, too, and he liked it all very much. Alia was wanting some tea now. She ordered the tea from Leaf. Caen ordered some tea, too, although he ordered a different tea. They relaxed. Alia felt full and complete. Caen turned to her and said, "Perhaps now I can introduce you to another portion of Serenity."

Caen

CHAPTER 6

TOLOV, THE LEADER

Alia and Caen walked away from their tables and chairs. It was so light out. It was like daylight, but she couldn't see any sun. Alia walked outside into a serene space. There were trees all around, but no people. She didn't see any people. They walked further, and again, saw many trees and further was a blue lake. All around, everything was so beautiful and peaceful.

Alia turned to Caen. "I feel so calm. Please explain to me about Serenity."

"Things are very calm here. There's no war. People are very calm. We do work, but it's not like work. It's our life. We love it. We don't work every day. Like you, we have several days off where we do wonderful, totally fun things. Although, our work is very fun. We take care of each other, but we are very independent. We make sure each other is cared for, and we live peacefully here, in SERENITY."

"There are no wars?" Alia asked.

"That's true." Caen said honestly. "There are no wars. At one time. There were many wars and very little peace. We had a very big war. Most of our people were in that war. We learned the hard way. We didn't really like ourselves. So, we made a pact, each one of us in Serenity, that we will no longer harm ourselves. We will no longer harm others. That's why our home is called SERENITY."

Alia sadly said, "Where I live, there's constant war."

Caen said, "Yes. I know."

Alia said, "I don't know how we can stop."

Caen said, "You and your people can. We did. We stopped. And we're in peace. We find things that challenge us, and things we are learning to do. It's not as though we don't learn and do things. But, when one of us needs some help, we have only to imagine it, and something or someone is there to help us. We're constantly learning new ways to be in life. It's called PEACE. We marry. We have children—all you experience where you live, we also experience. But, we have the precious gift of PEACE in SERENITY."

Alia looked at Caen. It was beyond her imagination. And yet, she liked the idea of peace and serenity very much. She said, "Will I meet some of your people?"

"Oh, yes," he said. "You will meet a lot of our people in a lot of different areas of Serenity, but we have no war."

Amazed by his words, Alia was awed, "That's quite a big thing."

He said, "Wait and see. You will learn a lot from the beings here. You will learn a lot from just being here. Wait and see."

Alia and Caen walked a little further. All of a sudden, a being appeared a slight distance from them.

"Oh," Caen said, "That is Tolov and he is our leader. He is a brave man, and lots of fun.

He's really lots of fun. Let's go up and I will introduce you to him. You'll like him a lot."

Alia said, "Okay, let's go."

They walked to meet Caen's leader. Caen introduced Alia to Tolov.

Tolov the Leader

Alia said, "You have an unusual name."

"Yes," he said, "I guess I do. People here have unusual names. Serenity embraces everything here as it is. My purpose is to 'EMBRACE ALL'. I AM TOLOV. Please ask any questions about our home of SERENITY. I AM happy to assist you to answer your questions. I am very old with great LIGHT and LAUGHTER."

Alia laughed, "PEACE and SERENITY."

TOLOV knowingly said, "PEACE and SERENITY are extremely important, where our heart is always. We feel a sense of gratitude, of compassion on each day of life. That's who and what we are. We're here for ourselves and for others. We're here to enjoy LIFE. We are very simple but advanced in who we are."

Grateful, Alia said to Tolov, "I'm so very glad to be here, with Caen, to meet you. I feel honored."

Tolov said quietly, "We are all learning about our true self. I AM TOLOV and am always here Alia. Just call my name and I'll be with you immediately!"

Caen and Alia said good-bye to Tolov.

They walked a little bit further and saw a lovely house. It was very different from her home. The front blue door was built into the ground surrounded by so many flowers and trees and ---- lightness.

No other houses were surrounding it.

Chapter 7

Almira

Caen said, "This is my Mother's house. She's a beautiful woman; a lovely person. Perhaps, you'll stay with her. She invites people here often. You and she will get along very well.

Of course, you'll decide what's best for you."

So, they knocked on the front door. The blue door was wood with a big, oblong globe of glass in the middle. One could see through the globe.

This was a place of peace — a home with a heart. Home with a heart to welcome Alia.

Caen's Mother came to the door. His Mother was very beautiful. She had blonde hair with long curls to her shoulders, tied by a golden swirl pendant on the top of her head. She wore a very simple dress, although very different from the clothes worn at Alia's home. She dressed like Caen. Caen wore a shorter dress, like a robe or a toga. Caen's Mother's dress was much longer. Her dress came to her ankles.

She said, "Hi Caen, my son! I'm so happy to see you!"

His Mother had a happy expression on her face. "You brought a friend with you."

Caen introduced Alia to his Mother. "Alia is my friend. Alia, this is my Mother, Almira.

Alia would like a place in Serenity to stay for a while. I thought of you, Mother. You would enjoy each other's company. Alia needs to rest after her long travel to Serenity. Perhaps, she'll feel at home with you, Mother."

Almira smiled and said "Come in! Come in to my home!"

Alia said politely, "Your home is so beautiful. It's very beautiful and bright."

"Well, part of my home is sunny and part of my house is underground covered by our dirt, trees, plants and flowers. We live partly inside and partly outside our homes. Come inside while I make some tea for us. Would you like some scones? I know Caen likes my scones."

Alia smiled and said, "Thank you. Thank you very much."

They went into the living room. It was a large room, with a very comfortable couch. The couch was like the one at Alia's home. Caen stayed close to Alia. He wanted her to feel very peaceful. He made her feel welcome.

Alia's mother excused herself to go make their tea.

Caen turned to Alia and said, "I think you will be happy here."

Alia smiling at Caen and said, "You're right. It's peaceful here."

"While we're waiting for tea and scones, perhaps we'll walk through parts of Almira's home." They walked to the kitchen. Caen said, "Mother, I'm going to show Alia your home."

Caen's mother replied, "Great! I'll finish making the tea and bring the scones."

So, Alia and Caen went off and explored his mother's home. They came to a large room covered with many shelves of books.

Caen said, "These are books from many decades ago about Serenity. I know my mother will be very happy to share them with you, so please come in here any time you want and read any of the many books." The next room was a sitting room. It was a smaller room than the living room. It had couches and chairs and tables and lamps.

You just touched the top of the lamps and everything brightened up.

Alia thought, "Oh! That is very lovely." When they left the room, the lamps turned off. Before they left the room, Alia saw a mirror and looked at herself. Yes, indeed, she was now 18 years old and looked lovely, much older than the age of 12. Her face had a glow, like Caen's face which always glowed. A youthful glow. Alia felt something for Caen and his Mother. She didn't know how to explain it. She felt love and loved. It was a caring, not a concern, but a caring that they would always be her friends. Alia would be at total peace in Serenity.

Caen pointed to his Mother's room and it was a dream place. The huge area was separated into three lovely spaces for meditating, sleeping and bathing. Her room was amazing.

The bath area was large and contained a deep beautiful oval tub. She could take a shower or relax in the huge bath tub.

Alia said, "Your Mother must really love this room." Caen laughed, "She does. She spends time every day in this room." The bathing room was covered with glass and looked outside. When his mother was in the bathing tub, she was surrounded by sky and beautiful plants and trees.

It was amazing!

It was incredible!

Alia said, "This is a wonderful space."

Caen said happily, "Yes, my Mother likes bathing here very much. Let's go to the next room. That one will be yours if you wish."

A curtain enclosed the roof and sides of the room. Caen flashed his hand and the curtain disappeared to reveal the beauty outside in his mother's garden. "I love it," Alia said. "It's all glass."

Caen said, "Yes. It's easy to sleep in here. When the draperies are opened, you see what Serenity truly is. You see such beautiful flowers, plants and trees and the gentle waving of the grass in a breeze.

Look a bit further, you'll see a pool. It's a beautiful pool. We don't use anything in the water to disturb the water. You see, Serenity is 'living water' because the water is alive. The water takes care of itself so that it's perfectly clean, always renewed.

Our water is 'living water'. When you swim in our water, your body is renewed and very much alive. Now, you have a bathroom with a tub much like Mother's. The tub also has 'living water'. So, when you take a bath, you are bathing in 'living water'. All water faucets lead to 'living water'. You'll experience what 'living water' gives to your body.

It's best if we go to the kitchen now to visit and eat with my mother."

While going to the kitchen, Caen said, "I live closer to the city, in a building with several people. The buildings in the city are very attractive and functional, but my mother's home is really a gift to one's spirit."

Alia said, "What about your father?"

Alia noticed Caen became a little sad.

Caen said, "My father is gone now, and probably will not return here. I loved him very much, and my mother loved him very much. She still does love him, in a way, but it's best that he left. We're happy for him." That's all Caen said. He didn't say that he died. He didn't say how long his mother had been alone. He said nothing.

They walked back to the kitchen. Caen waited for Alia to sit down, and then he sat down. Immediately, his mother carried the cups of tea to their table. The tea cups were beautiful. The cups were very different than anything she had ever seen. Caen's mother had plates as well. Again, they were very different than what Alia was used to. The plates were irregularly-shaped, but they were so beautiful. The cups were the same way. It took two hands to hold the cup. The scones looked delicious with blueberries and butter. So, they ate scones and drank tea.

Then, Caen's mother began to talk. "Well, it's time to talk about some important things. Number One, do you wish to live with me in my home?" Alia said, "Your home is very lovely. You are kind and very loving. So much peace here. Yes, I would love to stay with you, Thank you. I'm very happy to help in anyway. Please let me know."

Almira, Caen's Mother

Caen's mother said, "Of course. We'll play with the work, because that's the way work is done here. It's very much like play. I'm very happy to have you with me. In fact, I wish Caen could live with me, but I'm too far from the city for him to work daily. He must live where he needs to live. Truthfully, it's probably best for him, too, because he's learning his own way about things."

Almira said," I'm very happy to share my home with you, Alia. Caen will go back to his home in the city now. Whenever you wish, just think of him, and he will be here with you. That is our promise."

So, Caen said his goodbyes and left for his home. Alia stayed with his Mother.

Alia didn't have any fresh clothes or anything. She mentioned it to Caen's Mother. Caen's Mother said, "You will find some clothes here. I have many things, and you are welcome to them. We'll look at my clothes and you will choose what you would like to wear." So, they walked into Alia's new bedroom.

Caen's mother said, "Do you like this room."

Alia said, "Your home is a wonderful place. Your property outside is amazing!"

Almitra said, "Now, what was I thinking about? Oh well, it's not important. Sometimes I just forget. Oh, I'll bring you some clothes. Alia see what you would like to wear." Almira went into her own room. She selected three outfits. They were long togas, bright and colorful. She was about Alia's size.

Alia's spirit soared when Almira brought the togas – a yellow, blue and a pink/rose one. Almira said, "Are these togas your colors and will they fit you?"

Alia exclaimed "They're exquisite."

Almira said, "Well, I have many clothes. These are new and perhaps you would like to have them."

"Today, I'll wear the pink-rose toga. It's lovely. Thank you."

Almira said, "Good! We'll find sandals to match your pink toga."

So, Almira left and Alia looked at the togas. They were all so exquisite.

The toga was covered by a see-through rose color fabric with an underlying silk pink fabric. A gold pin was attached to the left shoulder of the toga. An exquisite rope-like structure went around the waist of the garment.

Almira said, "You look so lovely." The sandals Almira brought were comfortable, a silver-gold color and they fit Alia's feet perfectly.

Alia suddenly thought about Obi.

Alia said, "Before I came to Serenity, I met a fuzzy friend, Obi. He was very kind to me. He always protected me and made me feel very safe. I hope to see him again."

A special light came to Almira's eyes, "He seems like a unique being. I can sense him through your thoughts Alia. He is very kind and a special friend. You'll see Obi again."

Alia said, "I ate those wonderful scones, but I'm hungry again. I don't know why."

Almira said, "It's because you've traveled so far, and yes, you should eat something now. How about some soup? Why don't you help me? Afterwards, let's go to another floor in my home and create a project. Later, you can rest, or we could go into the city. You decide what you want to do. We are close to the city. I have two beautiful horses to ride into the city."

Alia said, "Horses are beautiful, but I can't ride."

Almira said, "You'll see. You'll love these horses, and you'll be able to ride. I promise."

Alia said, "Well, all right. I'm afraid but I'll **trust** that everything will be fine."

Almira said, "**Trust** is all you need in Serenity."

CHAPTER 8

TRUSTING ONE'S HIGHER SELF

After lunch, they went to the second floor in Almira's home. Again, everything was so beautiful, so light.

Almira explained, "In this room, I do something very special. I create remedies to help heal people using guidance from my **HIGHER-SELF**. HIGHER-SELF exists in all of us. You cannot see the HIGHER-SELF, but it is always with you, my dear. It takes **BELIEF** and **TRUST** in yourself to sense the HIGHER-SELF.

The HIGHER-SELF knows **PURE LOVE** and guides me in creating remedies of PURE LOVE in small vials. I just **KNOW** what is needed and what is to happen. Take, for instance, Caen. He's a very special being to me. He is my son. I love Caen very much. Occasionally, I feel his sadness. It's because his father is gone from our world now, and Caen feels very sad about this. Truthfully, it's hard for Caen to understand and not good for his physical body.

I've come to respect that my husband has gone on. Yes, he's gone having died in this dimension, yet he's very alive in another dimension. I know that he is happy in that other dimension.

I am grateful to know these things. It took many years to accept this truth. Caen hasn't totally accepted this truth. Each time we are together, Caen is better, but not at peace yet. He still has some sadness when he needs his father. My HIGHER-SELF responds through me, by making Caen a physical remedy that relieves his suffering a bit. I make this remedy in a vial. It's a small bottle containing a dropper.

There is a special flower from a Serenity plant that helps healing flourish. I use my fingers to squeeze the juice from the flower into the vial and then I push the flower into the vial. I then fill the *vial* with our 'living water'. When Caen feels sadness, he takes a dropper full of the healing remedy under his tongue. He breathes very deeply with his HIGHER-SELF in his mind. In that moment, he is suddenly happy again and forgets his sadness for a time. I can show you how to make Caen's remedy, if you would like."

Alia happily agreed to learn how to make Caen's healing remedy which was full of PURE LOVE.

Alia plucked the pink flower and squeezed the flower into the vial with PURE LOVE.

Then, she drew the 'living water' from the sink faucet into the vial, filling it.

Alia said, "It's very easy to create the remedy requested by the HIGHER-SELF and I am happy to make this remedy for Caen."

Almira said, "You can give this vial to Caen today. Perhaps we'll see other rooms in my house at a later time."

Alia said, "Thank you. Let's go to the city now."

Almira walked to the tiny stable behind her home and brought out two saddled horses for them to ride. One horse was tall and the other horse was much smaller. Both horses were black with white streams on the nose and the ankles.

Almira mounted her tall horse and motioned for Alia to mount the smaller horse. A wooden step just the right height helped Alia to mount her horse. Her pink toga made it easy for horse riding.

Alia was afraid of riding the horse because it was her first time.

Almira said, "Well, my dear, it's very simple, but it's important to follow my horse. Your horse is trained to never leave you alone. It's always with you and caring of you.

TRUST is all you need. Let's ride quietly now."

"All right. I'll ride this horse." Alia took the reins and sat straight up on the horse.

They quietly rode into the city. Almira's horse led and they rode slowly.

Almira then turned to Alia and said, "Okay now, we can ride a little bit faster if you are comfortable?"

Alia did feel very comfortable and loved riding. She felt a sense of freedom. The horse was very gentle. They headed toward the city. Within a short time, they arrived in the city.

Almira said, "Now we'll unsaddle the horses. It's a very lovely place. The horses like it a lot. There's a roof over their heads to protect them from the sun or rain. They look out onto the beautiful blue lake. We'll visit Caen. Then start our shopping."

The city felt alive. Alia could tell many people lived here. The buildings were very long and shaded by many trees. Alia wanted to see everything.

Almira said, "We'll see my son first. Just call his name in your heart. Caen will show up."

Alia gently called his name. "Caen," she said, "I'm here with your mother and we would like to see you." She turned around and Caen was smiling. He looked at Alia with love and happiness in his eyes.

Alia felt very good. She smiled at Caen. "We have a gift for you. With your mother's help, I made it with PURE LOVE." She opened the little bag containing the vial. "Here it is." she said happily. Caen looked at the vial and he smiled. He actually laughed. He was happy.

Caen smiled and said, "Yes. I really need this now. Thank you, Alia, for making it."

Almira said, "Alia's learning how to channel the contents of the vial from her HIGHER-SELF. Of course, she is a sensitive like you are a sensitive, Caen. Her whole body is sensitive, but then, Caen, you knew that. So, we made the remedy today. We thought of you when we made it. You know what it is. You've taken it before. It's about a week's worth. That's what it will take. You'll be very happy with the healing remedy, Caen. It is silent happiness. It is silent peace. It is joy."

Caen said, "I believe you my dear Mother. I'm very grateful. For some reason, when thinking of my father, I feel very sad that he's not here now."

Almira looked lovingly at her son and said, "I understand, my son but, you won't need to have this healing remedy forever. Eventually, you won't need it at all. We'll be together with your father in our hearts.

He's in a different dimension now. Although, his body looks pretty much the same as you remember, he thinks of you with love. Only love. You can always talk to him in your thoughts and he will respond to your thoughts. We both love him. We both know that he is happy in his new dimension. We are going shopping, but you can come if you want."

Caen said, "There are other things that I must do. It's best that I leave to do them now."

Chapter 9

Independent +
Interdependent
= Oneness

It was a beautiful day. As they walked further into the city, they saw people finally. All the people were happy and serene.

Alia stood back. She stopped walking. She looked around her. She just couldn't find the word for it, but something inside her was bothering her. Outside everything looked at peace and alive. People were walking. Some people were working. They were so friendly and peaceful.

Somehow, she just didn't feel right inside.

Almira turned to her and said, "Alia, is there something wrong?"

Alia didn't know what to say. How could she say that something needed her attention when everything on the outside looked so good, so peaceful, so perfect?

Alia turned to Almira and said, "I don't understand why I feel like this."

Caen's mother looked at her and said, "Is there something you are feeling INSIDE?"

Alia said, "Yes, I don't know exactly what I'm feeling, but INSIDE feels very restrictive."

Almira said, "Ah, I understand. This is something very important to you. Perhaps we should go back to my house."

Alia said, "Yes. Just all of a sudden it's best to go back to your home."

Almira said, "Let's go now. We'll come to the city again at another time. Let's go back to our horses."

They went back to saddle the horses. Caen's mother helped Alia climb on her horse. They glided away. It was still a beautiful day. Alia was very quiet now. So, they went slowly back to the house.

Alia excused herself and went to her room to lay down on her bed. She fell asleep and dreamed. In her dream, her inner voice told her to listen carefully, because what her inner voice said next was important— very important. Alia's inner voice said, "You, Alia, are wonderfully independent.

Each person is INDEPENDENT and yet, INTER-DEPENDENT and in ONENESS.

Each person must follow their own inner voice. Each inner voice is slightly different than their neighbors' inner voice but always supports the ONENESS OF HUMANITY.

You will hear many outer voices, and though those voices may be kind and loving, the messages may not be best for you. The outer voice is another's voice. The inner voice is your own voice.

We can only follow our own inner voice.

We listen to what people outside of us say, but it is important to respond only to our own inner voice.

If our inner voice disagrees with the outer voice, then we must wait and test again to see if our inner voice agrees with the outer voice.

If the inner voice says something is important for us to do, we must do it. We cannot work from others' needs. We must work only from what we feel is important."

That was all the inner voice said. We must follow our own inner voice.

Our own inner voice, our truth, never hurts us and never hurts another person.

If we have any reservations about what our inner voice says on a subject, then we must stop and do nothing.

Alia, listened to the important messages coming from inside her.

Alia slowly awoke from her dream and remembered what her own inner voice said—to follow her own inner voice, which may or may not agree with outside voices.

.

Chapter 10

Serenity's Essence

Alia was completely awake now. She felt alive. She was a little concerned, but she felt so alive—so very, "ON". She couldn't understand it. She felt liked she had slept a full day, but she got up and looked at the clock. She had only slept twenty minutes. She was quite surprised. She looked all around her. Everything glowed. It was always beautiful. But everything was shaded-blue—just a little blue, but it was her color. She knew that now.

She needed to follow her own inner voice, and as long as she followed her voice, that shade of blue would surround her. Otherwise, there would be beautiful colors around her, but not the slightly blue color. So, she got out of bed and looked in the mirror. She thought, "Maybe I'll comb my hair." Her long and flowing hair was a slight blue shade. Alia thought, "That too is interesting." Alia smoothed the wrinkles from her clothes and went to Almira.

Almira was in the kitchen and looked and said, "How are you?"

Alia said, "Well, I feel different."

Almira said, "Ah, Alia your color is a slight blue. Nobody would notice it, but I do because I've seen these things before. You're slightly blue."

Alia looked at Almira and said, "I had a dream. Now, I'll follow my inner voice, always.

The outside voices are neither good or bad, but they are not for me. I must follow my own inner voice that makes my color slightly blue."

Almira looked softly at Alia and said "You have learned a very, very important lesson. If you look at me deeply, you will see my color is rose. Nobody really ever notices, but I do. It's very important to follow you own inner voice. Others may think, 'Well, it's strange what Alia thinks.' But you must follow your own inner voice Alia, not, anyone else's voice."

Alia said, "Thank you," and she walked to the living room where she could sit and look at the beautiful mountains. Her inner voice said "All is well, Alia. Just look at the mountains." Alia looked at the mountains and felt quietly and completely comforted. Her inner self said, "Quiet comes from your SOUL." Alia thought, "The slight blue shade surrounds me now."

Alia was quiet for a very long time.

Almira quietly left Alia in the living room. She went into her meditative place in her own bedroom.

Both Alia and Almira were hearing and feeling their own inner voice guidance.

After a bit, Alia brought her attention back from the mountains. Almira came into the living room.

Almira said, "We could eat something now."

Alia said, "Eating! Sounds great! I'm really hungry."

Almira walked to the kitchen. She filled two bowls with some kind of grain and something that looked like milk. They ate the grain and milk and drank a special tea. Alia felt at peace and totally refreshed.

Alia said, "Perhaps we can go outside for a walk now." They noticed everything was so green with little flowers all around. Such beauty in the tiny flowers.

Almira said, "Let's go north from my home."

So, they went north. There wasn't really a road, but there was a pathway with many animals and purple-colored birds. A light, a pure white light glowed. Alia felt joy in her heart. She looked around. She looked on the ground, and she saw a rabbit. It had a blueish tint and was eating leafy greens. The rabbit suddenly looked up at Alia.

In her mind, she heard the rabbit say "Hello" or some type of greeting. Alia suddenly felt love from the rabbit. So, she gave the tiny rabbit what he gave her, LOVE.

Alia said "People from my home don't understand what LOVE really is."

Almira and Alia walked further, and then she saw a BEING. The BEING seemed like a human. The BEING said, "Alia my name is <u>SERENITY</u>. I give voice to the dimension in which you currently find yourself."

<u>SERENITY</u> is a beautiful angelic being surrounded by a bright white light, and gentle and compassionate love.

<u>SERENITY</u> smiled and walked beside Alia.

Alia turned to Almira, "Now, everything looks very different to me."

Almira answered gently but quite strongly, "Alia, you finally realize inside yourself what Serenity really is. The flowers, the grass, the animals look very unusual because they are LOVE, everything now is LOVE in SERENITY."

There was a quiet surrounding them now. Alia realized the place Serenity was very different. She sat on a large stone quietly. It was hard even to believe this place was real for her. She was amazed and shocked! But, it was a type of shock that was different than she had known before. It was a wonderment.

'What it would be like to live in this world'. It was so different. It was a miracle!

She exclaimed, "Everything is different from my home which is at war now. Very different. Is there a step that I've taken that's put me here? Can people from my home world join me in this place?"

<u>SERENITY</u> replied, "Yes, your people can learn to live like we do."

Well, Alia finally decided, after she had been through this experience, she needed to share this new life with Alee and her parents at her home.

Alia loved living in Serenity. She wanted to learn more about <u>SERENITY</u>.

Alia kissed and thanked Almira for everything.

The Essence of Serenity

Finally, Alia felt a deep need to return to her home, despite the war and terror. She knew that she would return to Serenity again in the future.

Alia told Almira, "I need to go back to my home world. Serenity is truly an amazing place, but I need to go to my home now. I can't even say why, but I miss my mother very much, and I need to go back home where there is war."

Almira said, "I understand. It's important to go home now. Caen can help you to go back. Okay?"

Alia said, "Thank you very much."

They walked back to Almira's house. Almira thought of Caen and he showed up immediately at Almira's home.

"Caen, Alia needs to go back to her home world now." Caen understood and smiled.

Alia said, "We'll be together again. Thank you for all you've shared."

So, they walked away from Almira's beautiful home and suddenly saw Tolov again.

Tolov said, "Oh, Alia, are you going back to your home world now?"

Alia said, "I've had a tremendous time here but I must go back to my parent's home where the war is happening."

Tolov understood completely why Alia must leave Serenity. "We gather your presence to us and expect to see you again in the very near future."

CHAPTER 11

FIRST TRANSFORMATION

She looked back at Serenity with gratitude.

When she turned back Caen was a merman now in the lake. He waved for Alia to jump into the lake.

Caen kissed the top of Alia's forehead. "You are a special being and loved very much. I'll be waiting here for your return."

Under the water, Caen and Alia no longer breathed. They were fine without breathing. Caen swum very deeply now and Alia fell asleep immediately. As Alia awoke she saw the whale. The whale said, "I can promise that you'll come back to Serenity. I bless you."

So, they gently acknowledged the blessing and swam toward their destination. Before long, they surfaced on the beautiful blue lake. Obi, the being that was hairy and about three feet tall, met her.

Caen kissed Alia, not wanting to let her go now. Inside, Caen felt immense love for Alia. Caen gently helped her out of the blue lake.

Her friend Obi waved to the merman and said to Alia, "Okay, I'll take you back to your home. Just follow me. Take my hand. It will be very easy and very sweet to go to your home world now. We all love you very much."

His partner, Lilly, joined him. They both took one of Alia's hands, and they started walking into the forest together.

Suddenly, she saw her puppy. She picked her puppy up in her arms saying, "I'll be back to be with you soon."

The puppy hopped from her arms and stayed by her legs. Her two fuzzy friends and the puppy were beside Alia.

Obi said, "We'll see you soon."

Alia and Caen

Epilogue

Inner Truth

Alia woke up instantly.

Alee was sitting beside her. "I was getting worried, you were sleeping so long, but you're okay now, that's all that matters to me. I've missed you, but I didn't want to wake you up. I felt you needed sleep."

Alia turned to Alee and said, "I love you Alee. I love you very much. But, I need to go home now. Do you want to go with me?"

Alee said, "Of course I'll go with you, anywhere you are, I'll be there."

He hugged her very tightly and meaningfully.

They started walking to their home. Eventually they could hear fighting but they were still very grateful to see their family again. They were finally at their family's home. Their mother and father were so happy and smiled with love at Alia and Alee.

Alia trusted her true inner guidance.

Now, Alia would always follow her inner voice. She'd always be safely guided and know her INNER TRUTH in each moment.

Printed in the United States
By Bookmasters